Notes for Parents

From a very early age, children enjoy learning the names of familiar objects around them. Talking about the things they use and play with helps them develop language, which is such an important element in all learning.

Once children are able to recognize real objects, the next step is to recognize the same things in pictures. The *First Hundred Words* has been imaginatively and carefully designed to help young children take this vital step. All the pictures are clearly placed in a proper setting to make this task easier.

There are three main stages in a child's development; first, before children can talk they are able to recognize the names of things. You can say "Bring me your cup" and you will often receive the right response. Second, children gradually learn to say the names. It is surprising how many new words children learn every day. Third, children learn that real objects can be represented by pictures. Encourage learning by playing a simple game. Ask your child to name an object in the book and then find, or point to, the real thing. The association between the real object and a picture of the object is most important.

Always praise your child's efforts. It gives them a real sense of achievement to be able to identify more and more pictures. Little children love getting things right. The *First Hundred Words*, with such highly motivating, colorful pictures will encourage children to succeed.

This is a lovely book for babies, toddlers and young children to return to again and again. Learning the first hundred words will be a first milestone. Share it with them and enjoy it together.

Betty Root

Usborne
First hundred words

Heather Amery
Illustrated by Stephen Cartwright

Language Consultant: Betty Root

Edited by Jenny Tyler

Designed by Mike Olley and Jan McCafferty

 There is a little yellow duck to find in every picture.

The living room

Daddy

Mommy

boy

girl baby dog cat

3

Getting dressed

shoes

underwear

sweater

4

undershirt   pants   t-shirt   socks

The kitchen

bread   milk   eggs

apple

orange

banana

Cleaning up

table

chair

plate

8

 knife  fork  spoon  cup

q

Play time

 horse

 sheep

 cow

10

hen   pig   train   blocks

41

Going on a visit

Granny

Grandpa

slippers

coat

dress

hat

The park

tree flower swings ball

14

slide   boots   bird   boat

15

The street

car

bicycle

plane

truck
bus
house

Having a party

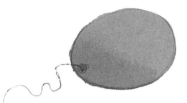
balloon

cake

clock

ice cream   fish   cookies   candy

19

Going swimming

arm

hand

leg

 feet

 toes

 head

 bottom

21

The changing room

mouth   eyes   ears

nose   hair   comb   brush

23

Going shopping

red   blue   green

24

yellow   pink   white   black

Bath time

soap

towel

toilet

26

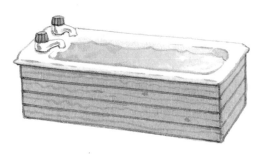  

bathtub tummy duck

Bed time

bed

lamp

window

door   book   doll   teddy bear

Match the words to the pictures

apple
ball
banana
book
boots
cake
car
cat
clock
cow
dog
doll
duck
egg
fish

fork

hat

ice cream

knife

lamp

milk

orange

pig

socks

sweater

table

teddy bear

train

undershirt

window

Counting

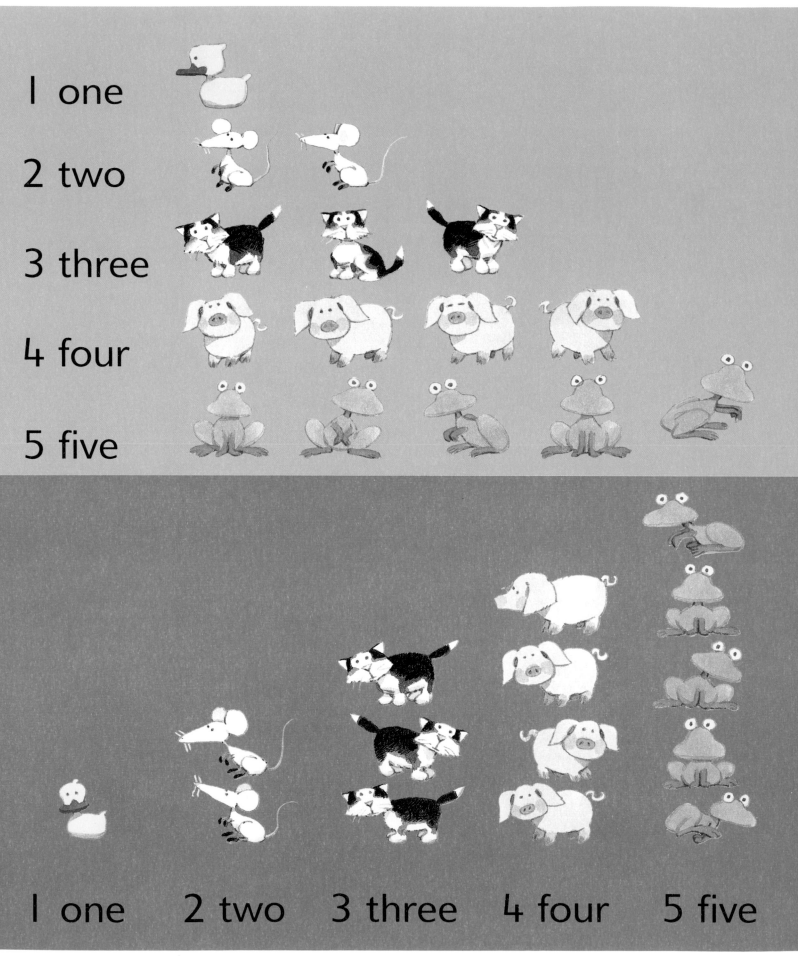

1 one

2 two

3 three

4 four

5 five

1 one   2 two   3 three   4 four   5 five

This edition first published in 2001 by Usborne Publishing Ltd, Usborne House, 83-85 Saffron Hill, London EC1N 8RT, England.
www.usborne.com
Copyright © 2001, 1988 Usborne Publishing Ltd.